In the early 1940s, a loving father crafted a small blue wooden engine for his son, Christopher. The stories this father, the **Reverend W Awdry,** made up to accompany the wonderful toy were first published in 1945. Reverend Awdry continued to create new adventures and characters until 1972, when he retired from writing.

Tommy Stubbs has been an illustrator for several decades. Lately, he has been illustrating the tales of Thomas and his friends, including *Tale of the Brave, Sodor's Legend of the Lost Treasure, The Great Race,* and *Journey Beyond Sodor.*

THOMAS & FRIENDS™

Thomas and the Beanstalk

By Christy Webster

Illustrated by Tommy Stubbs

Random House 🏠 New York

Thomas the Tank Engine & Friends™

CREATED BY BRITT ALLCROFT

Based on the Railway Series by the Reverend W Awdry
© 2018 Gullane (Thomas) LLC.
Thomas the Tank Engine & Friends and Thomas & Friends are trademarks of Gullane (Thomas) Limited. Thomas the Tank Engine & Friends and Design Is Reg. U.S. Pat. & Tm. Off. © 2018 HIT Entertainment Limited. All rights reserved. Published in the United States by Random House Children's Books, a division of Penguin Random House LLC, 1745 Broadway, New York, NY 10019, and in Canada by Penguin Random House Canada Limited, Toronto. Random House and the colophon are registered trademarks of Penguin Random House LLC.
rhcbooks.com   www.thomasandfriends.com
ISBN 978-0-399-55867-2
Printed in the United States of America
10 9 8 7 6 5 4 3 2 1
Random House Children's Books supports the First Amendment and celebrates the right to read.

HIT entertainment

It was the end of a very busy day on the Island of Sodor. The engines were settling down in their Sheds for the night. Thomas the Tank Engine thought that it would be nice to tell his friends a bedtime story. He told James and Percy his favorite fairy tale—*Jack and the Beanstalk*.

"I like the part about the magic beans!" Percy peeped when the story was over. "I wish a magic beanstalk would grow here on Sodor."

"Do giants like railway engines?" James wondered.

The next day, Thomas picked up a load from the farm—sacks of beans! Thomas chuckled. "Just like in my bedtime story!" he peeped.

Suddenly, Diesel 10 appeared around a bend. He was speeding out of control!

"Get out of my way, little toy tank engine!" Diesel 10 roared.

Thomas couldn't move fast enough. Diesel 10 bashed into him and raced off.

Thomas crashed into a side rail and tipped over. Some of his cargo spilled out of the trucks.

Thomas awoke, dazed and confused. He noticed some beans scattered in the grass next to the tracks. Suddenly, a tiny leaf shot straight out of the ground. Right before Thomas' amazed eyes, the tiny leaf grew and grew into a big plant, and then into a towering beanstalk, stretching high up into the sky! "Those must have been magic beans after all!" Thomas exclaimed.

Thomas could hardly believe it. The giant beanstalk was different from the one in his story—it had railway tracks circling all the way up to the top!

Thomas wasn't sure what he should do. This was a little scary! But he decided to be brave. He would ride up those tracks to see what was at the top of the beanstalk.

Thomas started up the beanstalk. Around and around and up and up he climbed—and then he climbed some more. It seemed like the beanstalk went on forever!

Finally, Thomas reached the top. He saw an amazing sight!

There, up above the clouds, Thomas discovered a giant, magical world! The flowers, the grass, even a set of tracks leading up to a huge castle, made Thomas feel very small, like a child's toy engine!

"Bust my buffers!" he gasped. "Everything's so big!"

Thomas couldn't help wanting to explore. He followed the tracks into a castle courtyard. There, he realized he was traveling on a Sodor-sized railway!

All the buildings, trees, and railroad signs were just the right size for Thomas. It was a toy train set!

Thomas looked up and around at the castle, with its impossibly high gates and turrets. "Why is everything else so big?" he wondered aloud.

Then Thomas heard the sound of a steam whistle.

The whistle was the most beautiful Thomas had ever heard. It sounded almost musical! He looked around, but couldn't tell where it was coming from.

At that moment, the ground beneath him began to shake. Thomas tried to hide behind what looked like a huge flower. But when it lifted up and flew away, Thomas saw that it was an enormous butterfly! Suddenly, a gigantic foot landed in front of him.

Thomas looked up and up and saw a man towering over
the entire courtyard. He was a giant—just like the giant from
Thomas' bedtime story!

Thomas had never seen anyone this big! Before he could
make a move, he heard a little voice calling to him.

"Quick! Over here!"

Thomas turned and saw a gleaming gold steam engine on
the track ahead of him. She was trying to get his attention.
He started to roll toward her, but before he could speak
to her, the giant reached down with his enormous hand
and picked up the little engine. Then he put her down on
another track.

The giant pushed the gold engine back and forth on the track. All the while, he made peep and whistle noises in his booming voice. Then Thomas realized—the giant was playing with the little engine as if she were a toy!

Suddenly, a loud horn blasted nearby. Thomas looked up and saw Diesel 10 approaching. He was enormous, too—big enough for the giant to ride in himself! The giant put down the gold engine and stomped over to the huge diesel.

Thomas saw his chance. He hurried over to the gold engine. "What is this place?" Thomas asked her.

"It's the giant's castle," the gold engine replied. "I don't like it here, and I want to get away."

She told Thomas that she had been taken from her home, where she was a very special engine. "I run on golden coal," she said. "But here, I'm just the giant's favorite toy. I wish I could go home."

Thomas wanted to help the gold engine. "I don't know how to get to your home from here, but I can take you back to mine," he said.

Thomas told her about the Island of Sodor, where everything was the right size for them. "You would be safe and happy there," he said.

"Sodor sounds wonderful!" the gold engine said.

"I climbed up a giant beanstalk to get here," Thomas said. "It's this way." He headed toward the courtyard gate. But after a few feet, he slowed and stopped.

He was out of coal! "I must have used it all up climbing the beanstalk!" he cried.

"Take some of my golden coal," the gold engine told him. "Quickly! I think I have just enough for both of us."

With the special gold coal in his hopper, Thomas felt magical! His pistons puffed faster than ever as he raced toward the gate, with the gold engine following close behind him.

At that moment, the giant made a loud sniffing noise. "I smell steam!" he said. He turned and saw the two little engines trying to get away. His thunderous voice boomed:
Fee-fi-fo-fum,
I see two engines on the run.
If they're toys, or if they're real,
I'll now have TWO engines to steal!

The giant and Diesel 10 chased after Thomas and the gold engine as they steamed out of the courtyard.

"Get back here, little toy tank engines!" Diesel 10's booming voice rang out.

Thomas sped up, heading toward the beanstalk. If they could just get back to Sodor, he knew everything would be all right!

Thomas and the gold engine barreled down, down, down the tracks, spinning around and around the beanstalk.

"We made it! We're on Sodor! We're home!" Thomas cried as they reached the bottom, feeling a little dizzy. But when the two engines looked up, they were shocked to see that the giant was coming down the beanstalk after them!

"Oh, no!" Thomas exclaimed. "Sodor is full of little engines. The giant will want us all for his toys!"

Thomas thought quickly. He backed up and bashed into the beanstalk with all his might. He saw his friends James and Percy in the distance and called to them for help.

Soon, all four engines were slamming into the beanstalk, over and over again, as hard as they could. Finally, it looked like the beanstalk and the giant were about to fall. Thomas closed his eyes, bracing for the crash. . . .

THUD!

Thomas opened his eyes as he felt himself being tugged. Two engines were pulling him upright. Percy and James were still there—but the little gold engine was gone! "What happened?" Thomas asked. "Where's the beanstalk?"

"Beanstalk?" Percy asked. "What beanstalk? We came to help when we heard about your crash with Diesel 10."

Thomas told his friends about everything that had happened—the beanstalk, the magical world above the clouds, the giant, and the special gold engine. "It all seemed so real," he said softly. "But it must have been a dream. . . ."

"I guess giants really do like railway engines, after all," James said with a chuckle.

"Thomas, look!" Percy said. Thomas' Driver was holding up a single piece of gold-colored coal he'd found in Thomas' hopper. The Driver looked puzzled.

"What is that?" James asked.

Thomas gasped. He didn't know what to say. Because it had all been a dream . . . hadn't it?